JEANNE BIRDSALL

Teaflet & Roog
Make a Mess

Illustrated by
JANE DYER

Alfred A. Knopf
New York

For Henry —J.B.

For Violet —J.D.

THIS IS A BORZOI BOOK PUBLISHED BY ALFRED A. KNOPF

This is a work of fiction. Names, characters, places, and incidents either are the product of the author's imagination or are used fictitiously. Any resemblance to actual persons, living or dead, events, or locales is entirely coincidental.

Text copyright © 2021 by Jeanne Birdsall
Jacket art and interior illustrations copyright © 2021 by Jane Dyer

All rights reserved. Published in the United States by Alfred A. Knopf, an imprint of Random House Children's Books, a division of Penguin Random House LLC, New York.

Knopf, Borzoi Books, and the colophon are registered trademarks of Penguin Random House LLC.

Grateful acknowledgment for Teaflet's song on page 48 goes to Angela DiTerlizzi.

Visit us on the Web! rhcbooks.com

Educators and librarians, for a variety of teaching tools, visit us at RHTeachersLibrarians.com

Library of Congress Cataloging-in-Publication Data is available upon request.
ISBN 978-0-593-17911-6 (trade) — ISBN 978-0-593-17912-3 (lib. bdg.) — ISBN 978-0-593-17913-0 (ebook)

The text of this book is set in 14-point New Veljovic Pro.
The illustrations were created using a 2H pencil on watercolor paper
and rendered in watercolor, colored pencil, and gouache.
Book design by Martha Rago.

MANUFACTURED IN CHINA
May 2021
10 9 8 7 6 5 4 3 2 1
First Edition

TO OUR READERS

Jane and Jeanne, who made this book together, are friends and neighbors. Jeanne wrote the story, and Jane used wire and wool to bring the story's characters to life. She fashioned the wire into a kind of skeleton, then covered it with wool from her own sheep, one layer at a time. Every layer had to be repeatedly poked with a special needle to compact the wool. This is called needle-felting.

Jane made all the clothes, even the shoes and hats. She also designed the rooms (sometimes Jeanne helped) and made lots of what went into them, such as the cookbook and the braided rugs, plus the *delicious* cakes and pies, which she sculpted from clay. Everything was carried around the corner to Jeanne's shooting studio, where she and Jane set up the scenes on a small stage, using pins and string to help characters who had trouble holding a pose. When a scene was just right, Jeanne photographed it.

You'll also find watercolors in this book. Jane painted them, with no help at all from Jeanne.

ONE

✤*Chances are* you've never found Trelfdom, because wherever you look, it's always somewhere else. Across the river, maybe, or in a different wood, or at the bottom of the hill. Until you cross the river, explore that other wood, or climb down the hill, and discover that Trelfdom isn't there, either.

If you haven't found Trelfdom, you've never visited a certain cozy little higgledy-piggledy house that sits halfway up an enormous tree. This is where Roog and his sister, Teaflet, live. Or, rather, where Teaflet and her brother, Roog, live. I say it both ways around, to keep from offending anyone.

Despite being small, Teaflet and Roog are the same as any other sister and brother, happy together until something goes wrong. Except that what goes wrong for them isn't what usually goes wrong for most of us.

You see, Roog loves working in the kitchen: cooking, baking, anything to do with food. And Teaflet loves helping any creature who comes to her with a problem. Like the bluebird who was too shy to sing, and the baby hedgehog who didn't know how to uncurl. Teaflet's creatures never mess up Roog's food projects on purpose, but sometimes they just can't help it. The bluebird didn't understand that the blueberries on the counter were meant to be baked into muffins. It's not the kind of thing birds are taught by their parents. And I don't think it was the hedgehog's fault that Roog poured chocolate-cake batter on him. For a hedgehog, a cake

pan is a perfectly natural place for a nap. But these mishaps are rare, and life in the higgledy-piggledy house is mostly calm.

While everything that comes out of Roog's kitchen is delicious, he has a specialty—strawberry jam. Scrumptious, mouthwatering strawberry jam, sweeter and more berry-ish than any jam you've ever tasted. It's so yummy that once a year he and Teaflet have a big Strawberry Jam Party for their friends. You can eat the jam with cake, pie, pancakes, waffles, ice cream, toast, crois-

sants, pudding, tapioca—and even oatmeal, if anyone wants it, but no one ever does.

The party is always on the fifth Saturday after the first full moon after the strawberries ripen on the vine. Some say this is the easiest time for outsiders to find Trelfdom. I say they're wrong, and I'm the one to know. But it certainly is the best time to visit. If you're lucky enough to manage that, be sure to have a slice (or three—they're small, remember) of Roog's double-chocolate cake with strawberry jam. It's my favorite.

TWO

Roog was working in the kitchen, and had been since early morning. This year's Strawberry Jam Party was happening the very next day, and he still had mountains of food left to prepare. Up next was his lemon poppy-seed cake. He'd arranged the ingredients on the table—twenty-three poppy seeds, a lemon, flour, sugar, butter—but he couldn't begin yet. Teaflet was in his way.

And not just Teaflet, but also a wasp nest almost as big as a trelf. The nest contained no wasps, thank goodness, but it wasn't quite empty. A baby raccoon playing hide-and-seek had gotten her leg stuck in it. She was very young, and scared she'd stay stuck for the rest of her life.

"I'll get your leg out, I promise, and it won't hurt a bit," Teaflet told the raccoon. "But first take a sip of this calming tea. It'll help with your nerves."

The raccoon was shaking too hard to drink tea, and spilled most of it onto the floor. Roog wiped it up and drank the rest himself. He needed calming as much as the raccoon, maybe more. Preparing for the Strawberry Jam Party always made him tense, but this year he was in an absolute frenzy. It was going to be the tenth of these parties, and he wanted it to be the best ever. Maybe even ten times the best ever. Maybe even ten times the best ever of any party ever, whether or not strawberry jam was involved.

"Teaflet, how much longer will you be?" he asked. "It's impossible to work with you and that wasp nest in the middle of the kitchen."

9

"Just until the raccoon is relaxed enough for nest removal. You can't hurry these things."

DONG DONG DONG! That was the sound of the large bell hanging at the bottom of Teaflet and Roog's tree. It meant that a visitor was about to climb the long flight of steps up to their house.

"Who could that be?" wondered Roog.

"Maybe someone wanting an early taste of strawberry jam."

"Well, they can't have any. I'll tell them to go away." Roog never gave out jam before the party. "While I'm gone, be careful with the ingredients on the table, the ones for my lemon poppy-seed cake. I've got only twenty-three seeds, and I need every one of them."

"I'm always careful," said Teaflet. "You know that."

When Roog left, she made more calming tea. This time the raccoon drank it, and stopped shaking so hard.

"Ready for me to get you free?" asked Teaflet. "You hold tight, and I'll tug the nest. One, two, three, PULL!"

Nothing budged, neither the foot nor the nest. Teaflet was ready to try again when—*DING DING DING!*

 That was the sound of another large bell, this one hanging beside the front door.

It meant that the visitor had climbed to the top of the steps and reached the house. A moment later, Roog came running back into the kitchen, clutching a letter.

"It wasn't someone asking for jam, Teaflet. It's an

official letter from the new inspector of neatness!"

Trelfdom had many inspectors. There was an inspector in charge of tempers (trelfs were supposed to keep them), another in charge of hair (trelfs were supposed to have lots), another in charge of time (trelfs were supposed to make the most of it), and so on. Of all the inspectors, the most worrisome was the inspector in charge of neatness. The list of neatness rules—like how to make your bed, how to fold your clean clothes, how to roll up the tube of toothpaste—was a mile long and always getting longer. The previous inspector, Inspector Ash, had been reasonable, and had passed Teaflet and Roog despite the feathers on the living room floor. (The cardinal getting whistling lessons from Teaflet had dropped them there.) But this new one, Inspector Maple, had a reputation for being extra strict.

"Probably just another dumb rule for the list," said Teaflet. "Let's try again, baby raccoon. One, two, three, FOUR, pull! Nope, still stuck."

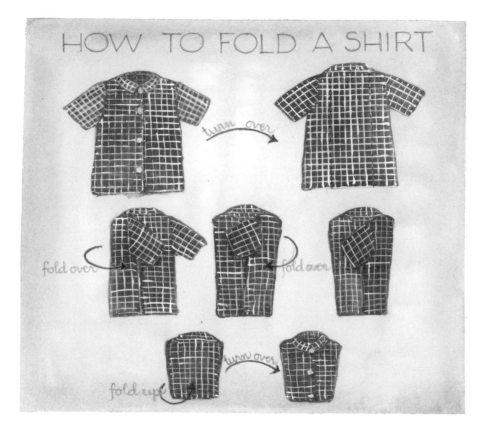

HOW TO FOLD A SHIRT

turn over

fold over

fold over

fold up

turn over

Roog tore open the envelope and groaned. "It's much worse than that! She's coming to inspect us early tomorrow morning, on the very day of our Strawberry Jam Party! I don't have time to clean the house now, not on top of all the food preparation!"

"So we'll fail, and pay the fine." With the old inspector, the fine had been seven trelf dollars. Teaflet and Roog had that much saved, and a little more.

Roog was back to reading the letter, and he groaned louder. "The rule has changed. We don't just have to pay a fine if we fail. We also have to spend the day cleaning Inspector Maple's house!"

"It's a racket."

"It's a disaster! If we're cleaning her house, we can't be having the Strawberry Jam Party. All our friends will be disappointed, and I'll never be happy again."

Discouraged, Roog sat down on the floor with a thump.

ATTENTION: TEAFLET & ROOG
THIS IS TO INFORM YOU THAT ON THE FIFTH SATURDAY AFTER THE FIRST FULL MOON AFTER THE STRAWBERRIES RIPEN ON THE VINE, I, INSPECTOR OF NEATNESS, WILL COME TO INSPECT YOUR HOUSE.
PLEASE BE ADVISED THAT I WILL BE CHECKING FOR THE FOLLOWING:
1. PROPERLY MADE BEDS.
2. NEATLY FOLDED CLOTHES.
3. TOOTHPASTE TUBES PROPERLY ROLLED.
4. CLEAN FLOORS AND RUGS.
5. POLISHED POTS, BELLS, & DOORKNOBS.
6. FOOD NEATLY MADE.
7. (NO) DIRTY DISHES.
8. (NO) ANIMALS.
9. (NO) DUST.
10. SHINY WINDOWS.
CHIP, CHOP, CHIP!

Inspector Maple
DEPARTMENT OF NEATNESS
TRELFDOM

THREE

Roog's thump was a big one, like this—*THUMP!* It startled the raccoon so much she yanked her leg right out of the wasp nest, then leapt up to the top of the refrigerator. Teaflet was thrown off balance and landed on the floor, with the nest on top of her. This wasn't so bad—she wasn't hurt. But she'd jogged the table when she fell, and the ingredients for Roog's lemon poppy-seed cake were flying every which way.

"My poppy seeds!" Roog was already on the floor, hunting for this most important ingredient. He inspected every crack and cranny, some so deep they could easily swallow a poppy seed.

"What happened?" The nest blocked Teaflet's view.

"Some of my poppy seeds are lost. I can find only sixteen."

"I'm sorry, Roog," she said.

"I can get more from Crarkie," he said. "Not that it matters anymore. After this inspection, there won't *be* a Strawberry Jam Party."

"Roog, we've got to try. You keep cooking, and I'll clean the house. I'll clean like I've never cleaned before. Inspector Maple won't find anything wrong, and she'll have to pass us."

Roog rolled the nest off her. "Do you really think so?"

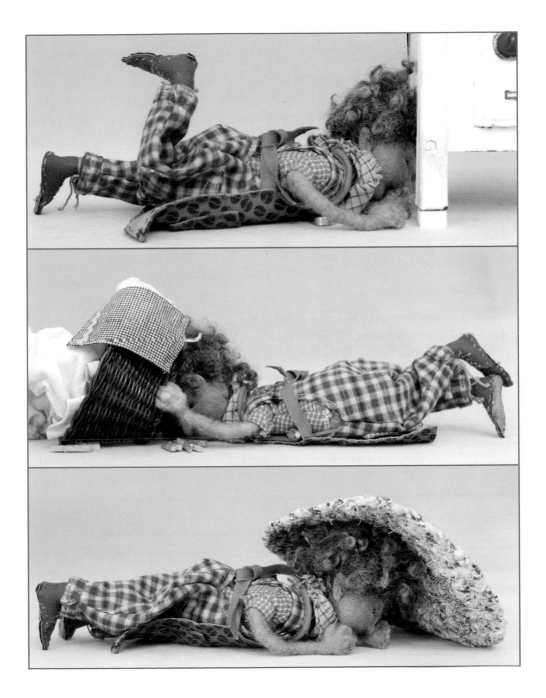

"Yes! I'll do the house top to bottom, scouring every inch."

"Thank you, Teaflet." Roog dropped his voice to a whisper to keep the raccoon from hearing. "You know what a mess your creatures make. If we're going to pass, the raccoon has to go away until the inspection is over. And you have to convince the bluebird to go, too."

"But the bluebird is still too shy to sing."

"I heard her singing opera," said Roog. "She's not shy—she just likes our laundry basket. And is the hedgehog still in your sock drawer?"

"Maybe." Teaflet knew he was.

"Anyone else?" Roog was right to ask. None of Teaflet's

creatures ever wanted to leave.

"Perhaps." The young pheasant who needed help with his strutting was in the spare bedroom, practicing in front of the long mirror.

"Please, Teaflet! For the Strawberry Jam Party! I'll get

rid of the wasp nest, if you could just get the creatures to leave."

"Okay, okay." It wasn't the creatures' fault that their fur and feathers fell off. But Roog was right. They made it hard to keep a house clean.

She got the raccoon off the refrigerator and took her along to see the bluebird, hedgehog, and pheasant. They were terribly sad to hear they'd have to leave, the pheasant most of all. Teaflet had never before seen a pheasant weep, and it was too much for her.

"Don't cry, please don't. I'll figure something out. Everyone, come sit on my lap—it helps me think."

The creatures did their best to get into her lap, except there wasn't enough room, and the bluebird ended up on Teaflet's head.

"I have a plan," she said finally. "Follow me, and don't make a sound. Nothing. Not a peep."

FOUR

✤ *The pheasant,* the hedgehog, the raccoon, and the bluebird followed Teaflet up a flight of steps, and then another and another, climbing higher and higher, until they reached the storage room at the top of the house. It had a large wardrobe where Teaflet and Roog kept their summer clothes in the winter, and their winter clothes in the summer. Plus a smaller cupboard, just for hats.

The storage room also held the boxes full of decorations for the Strawberry Jam Party. Balloons and bunting, twinkly lights and tablecloths, plates and mugs painted with strawberries, a large banner to string between two trees, and masses of confetti. The confetti was special this year, and Roog meant to toss it everywhere. The party would be as colorful as the food would be delicious.

"You can stay in here," Teaflet told the creatures. "Just don't touch anything, and please don't make any noise. If Roog can't hear you, he won't know you're here, and what he doesn't know won't worry him. Of course, you'll have to leave early tomorrow morning, before Inspector Maple arrives. You can come back later, after she's gone."

Teaflet opened the room's one window, to let in fresh air. Just outside were steps the hedgehog and raccoon could climb down in the morning. The pheasant and bluebird could fly.

"Have I thought of everything? Wait, I know—if you get thirsty, a bucket that catches rainwater is hanging on the branch out there, next to the steps," she said. "Please remember I'll have to clean in here after you leave to-morrow, so try not to make too much work for me."

One by one, the creatures came to her for hugs.

"Yes, I love you, and you too," she said. "Also you, and of course I love you, too. Now I have to go clean the house. Be kind to each other, and remember to be quiet. Quiet, quiet, quiet!"

Meanwhile, Roog was on his way to the best poppy garden in Trelfdom, in search of seven new poppy seeds. He wore a hat, hoping no animals would recognize him and ask to be taken home to see Teaflet. The animals recognized him anyway, but just one had a problem— a grasshopper who could jump only sideways. But she was enjoying the change and could wait until after the inspection to see Teaflet.

Crarkie was the trelf in charge of the poppy garden. She was happy to give Roog the poppy seeds, but first she wanted to talk about tomorrow's party.

"The tenth annual Strawberry Jam Party! Everyone is so excited," she said. "We're all skipping dinner tonight to leave room for the feast."

Roog didn't like the idea of his friends going hungry because he and Teaflet were cleaning Inspector Maple's house instead of giving a party. But he couldn't tell Crarkie about that possibility — panic

would spread throughout Trelfdom.

"Maybe you should have a little bit of dinner," he said. "You know, to help you sleep."

"Goofy Roog, always worried about nothing! Let's go to the garden for the poppy seeds."

There were plenty of seeds in the garden. There was also a mouse huddled on top of one of the poppies. A mouse with a problem — his tail was snarled in a mess of long grass and short sticks.

"I tried untangling him," said Crarkie. "But I think he needs Teaflet."

Not while she was cleaning the house for an inspec-

tion! But Roog's heart was softer than he let on. He just couldn't leave the sad little guy stuck on top of a poppy.

"You're too large for me to carry all that way in my arms," he told the mouse, "but if you can ride on my back, I'll take you to my sister."

The mouse didn't want to ride on anyone's back, but he'd heard about Teaflet and how kind she was. He slid off the poppy and onto Roog's back, and Roog fell down. He wasn't hurt, but his overalls got dirty.

"Doesn't matter," he said. "I've got other overalls. Let's try again."

This time Crarkie helped the mouse get settled, and Roog started the slow journey back home. Four more times he fell, once into a rotting mushroom. Oh, the smell! The mouse didn't get hurt or even dirty, but by the time they got home, Roog was worn out and very dirty indeed.

FIVE

Teaflet was sweeping the hallway when Roog brought the mouse inside.

"Dear mouse, how uncomfortable you must be!" she cried, putting down her broom. "And, Roog, what happened to you? Why do you stink? Are you wounded?"

"No, I'm not wounded, just dirty."

"Are you sure? I could bandage you." Teaflet loved bandages.

"Honest, there's nothing to bandage." Roog didn't love being bandaged. "Just take care of the mouse."

"Yes, that's quite a tangle he's in. I'll need your flax-seed oil to get out the knots."

"Make sure you leave some for the rest of my baking."

After Roog washed off the dirt and stink, and put on clean clothes, he decided to take a quick nap to recover. He stretched out on the living room rug and was dreaming about piecrust when he was shocked out of sleep by awful crashing noises. They were coming from the kitchen.

Roog didn't think this boded well. And, indeed, just as he opened his eyes, the mouse was zooming past, followed by a trickling stream of flaxseed oil.

"TEAFLET!" roared Roog.

She rushed into the room. "I'm sorry, Roog. The mouse was so pleased to be untangled he jumped onto the clothesline. Your dish towels fell down and knocked over the flaxseed oil bottle. I can wash your dish towels, but the flaxseed oil bottle is, well . . ."

"Empty?"

"I'm sorry," she said again. "I'm ruining everything."

Roog was polite enough not to agree with her. "I can get more flaxseed oil from Brigley. But you'll have to clean up the spilled oil. And the mouse has to leave!"

"I know." And Teaflet did know. She was taking a risk with four creatures in the storage room at the top of the house. She couldn't add another.

But when she took the mouse outside, his tail got tangled in the grass all over again. She just couldn't send him away, not like this. Really, were five creatures that many more than four?

She led the mouse around the tree and showed him the back steps. "When you get to the top, go through the window. I'll meet you up there."

Teaflet took the inside route, through the house, to the room at the top. When she got there, the pheasant, hedgehog, raccoon, bluebird, and mouse—who had just arrived—rushed over. They pushed her to the floor so they could sit in her lap. Maybe because they hoped she wouldn't notice what they'd done.

"You got into the confetti for the party," she said.

Everyone looked guilty, and also extra colorful. Even the mouse had picked up some, just from running across the floor. Now Teaflet was covered with it, too.

The confetti wasn't the only party decoration they'd gotten into. The twinkly lights and bunting were draped over the wardrobe. The tablecloths had been spread out and made into a tent, which wasn't empty. When Teaflet

opened the flap, she saw two newcomers: an owl and a baby bunny. They'd entered through the open window, of course. If the mouse could do it, so could anyone else. Why hadn't she thought of that before? She groaned, and was awfully glad Roog didn't know what was going on.

"This is too much for me. The owl and baby bunny

have to leave. Roog and I are in the middle of a crisis, and I can't take on any more—" Teaflet stopped. She couldn't send them off without helping them first.

The owl had a sore neck from too much head-spinning, and now his head was stuck facing backward. This was a more difficult problem than usual, and

Teaflet needed her skills with both massage and hypnosis to fix him up. Soon his head was back to working the way it was supposed to.

The baby bunny was a different matter altogether. She crawled crookedly across the floor, trying to look needy, her ears drooping. But Teaflet quickly discovered that she was perfectly healthy, and had come because she'd heard about creatures having fun in the room at the top of the house.

"They're not here to have fun! This is an emergency hideout to protect the Strawberry Jam Party!"

Teaflet had raised her voice. Now everyone was miserable, especially the pheasant, who started to cry again.

"I'm sorry. Please don't cry. You can all stay. But we're going to put away the party supplies, and please, please, don't touch them after that. And if anyone else tries to come in, tell them we're full up. They'll have to come back tomorrow—*after* the inspection."

SIX

✦*Meanwhile,* Roog was on his way to Brigley's house to ask for more flaxseed oil. He was wearing an even larger hat this time. It still didn't disguise him. All sorts of creatures waved and sent their love to Teaflet, but at least no one had a problem. Until the chipmunk, who wanted to talk to Teaflet about stress. Roog said, "You think *you're* stressed?" and felt guilty for the rest of the journey.

"Of course you can have flaxseed oil," said Brigley when Roog arrived. "Anything to help out with the Strawberry Jam Party. We've heard it's going to

be ten times the best jam party ever."

"Well, we can hope." Roog tried to look cheerful. "You never know when something can go wrong."

"Nothing will go wrong, Roog! What a worrier. Before you go, though, there's someone I want you to meet."

Brigley took Roog to the bottom of his tree and introduced him to a toad who lived there. A toad with a problem. She couldn't get her tongue to roll back into her mouth. It just stuck straight out, making her look peculiar.

"Can Teaflet help her?" asked Brigley.

Roog knew he should say no, and he even tried to. If there was another catastrophe in his kitchen, he'd never finish preparing the party food. But he felt even worse for the toad than he had for the mouse. And at least the toad could hop, and wouldn't have to be carried.

But Roog hadn't counted on how difficult it is to hop with a long tongue sticking out. It dragged in the dirt, got caught on low branches, and tripped up its owner. The toad tried walking backward, trailing the tongue behind her, but it was slow going.

"I'll carry your tongue for you, if you like." Roog knew he'd get dirty again, but he couldn't stand watching the toad struggle.

The toad offered up her tongue, Roog carefully took hold, and now they had a new problem. The tongue was ticklish in certain spots. Since Roog didn't know which spots, there was lots of extra jumping and skittering on the toad's part, and lots more falling into the dirt on Roog's part. The worst fall was just before they got home—into the stream. Yes, the water did wash off some of Roog's dirt, but the

dirt that didn't wash off was now mud.

When they went inside, Teaflet put down her scrub brush.

"Darling toad, your tongue!" she cried. "And, Roog, what happened to you this time?"

"Just dirt and stream water," he said. "I do *not* need any bandages."

"All right, calm down. Let me think about how to help the toad."

"Just stay clear of the table. All the ingredients for peach pie are on it, and if you wreck anything, I don't have time to get more."

"I'll be careful," she said. "You know how much I love peach pie. Maybe a song can help the toad."

"No, Teaflet, not one of your songs!" The last creature Teaflet had tried to heal with a song was a baby skunk. The house had just gone back to smelling normal.

"Song is the only thing that works in cases like these. Let me think for a minute. Ah! I've got it!" Teaflet began to sing—out of tune, like always.

> *You can't trill and you can't croak,*
> *And you look silly to the other folk.*
> *So roll it up, fold it up,*
> *Curl up your tongue.*
> *You can't have a meal*
> *Until the deed's done.*

Even with his hands over his ears, Roog could hear all the sour notes. By the second verse he was thinking about leaving the house until Teaflet stopped singing. But it was a good thing he stayed—at the end of the third verse, the song cured the toad. Her tongue suddenly rolled up—*SNAP!*—and into her mouth, where it belonged. She was so happy she started dancing along to Teaflet's song. And then Teaflet was dancing with her,

hopping and twirling. And then someone—neither ever admitted which it was—bumped into the table. The peach for the peach pies was now rolling, rolling, rolling . . .

"*Noooooooooo!*" Roog dove under the peach just before it landed. He was a little smashed, but the peach was fine.

"I'm sorry, Roog," said Teaflet. "Are your ribs broken? Do you need a bandage?"

"I do not—not—not need a bandage, but, Teaflet—"

"I know. The toad has to leave."

This time she knew that the toad really and truly did have to leave. There were already far too many creatures hidden upstairs. She walked and the toad hopped out of the house and to a lovely damp spot beside the stream.

"If it weren't for this inspection, I'd love to have you stay longer," said Teaflet. "But Roog cares so much about the party. You understand, don't you?"

The toad turned her back on Teaflet, and Teaflet sadly went inside.

FOOD TO MAKE
1. cakes
2. tarts
3. jam
4. bread
5. muffins
6. pudding
7. pies

SEVEN

For the rest of that day and into the night, Roog sifted, measured, stirred, buttered, smushed, whipped, sliced, grated, and baked. The kitchen filled up with pie after cake after bread after pudding after cookies, until there was no room left. Every surface was covered with delicious food.

Meanwhile, Teaflet swept, scrubbed, polished, tidied, bleached, aired out, dusted, and mopped. Not to mention having to launder and iron the clothes Roog had gotten dirty, plus some of her own, like the apron covered with confetti. At long last, she was done. Hoping she'd never have to clean again for the rest of her life, she went to the kitchen to cheer Roog on through his labors and clean up the last of his mess.

It was long past their bedtime when he iced the last

cake—double chocolate. He gave out a feeble hooray, tripped over Teaflet's broom, and fell asleep where he landed. Teaflet pulled the broom out from beneath him and slipped a pot holder under his head for a pillow. More than anything, she wanted to go to sleep beside him. But she had one last task—to remind the creatures upstairs about leaving early the next morning. Taking her cleaning supplies with her, she dragged herself up to the top of the house.

Once again everyone rushed to sit on her lap. This time she ended up flat on the floor, legs and arms sticking straight out, buried top to toe under creatures. The good news was that they'd put away all the party supplies, even the confetti. The bad news was that there were even more of them than before. Plus, they'd gotten into the hat cupboard, and everyone was wearing a hat.

"You're not supposed to be wearing hats," she said. "And there should be only seven of you. Line up, please. I need to count."

The seven she knew about came first—the pheasant, bluebird, hedgehog, mouse, raccoon, owl, and baby bunny. The rest of the line, which seemed to stretch on forever, was made up of newcomers. There was the skunk she'd sung to months earlier, the cardinal she'd taught to whistle, and the sideways-jumping grasshopper and stressed chipmunk Roog had met on

his travels. There were also four of the baby bunny's brothers and sisters, the toad—with her tongue still in her mouth—and a squirrel with a peach pit stuck on his nose. Teaflet recognized the peach pit. It was the one Roog had thrown outside after baking his peach pies.

"Seventeen of you? How did that happen? Seventeen is quite a crowd." She yawned. "My goodness, I'm tired. Please put away the hats while I help those who need it. Squirrel with the peach pit, you can go first, though maybe before we begin I could just shut my eyes for a

minute . . . just a teeny-weeny rest and I'll be . . . I'll be . . ."

The creatures waited, but there was no end to the sentence.

Teaflet had fallen asleep.

ZZZZZZZZZZZZ

EIGHT

 Teaflet stirred, then opened her eyes. Beside her, so close it almost touched her nose, was a dustpan, brimming with dust, dirt, fur, and one peach pit. Beyond the dustpan, standing in a clump, blocking the window, were the creatures. There seemed to be an additional baby bunny, but it hardly mattered at this point.

"Thank you for cleaning while I slept. Who helped?" she asked.

Everyone looked embarrassed.

"You all did? How kind of you. And who un-stuck the squirrel's peach pit?"

The pheasant did a little strut.

"You did a good job, pheasant. And I see everyone put away the hats. Thank you."

She smiled at the creatures—she did love them so—but no one smiled back. Indeed, now that they didn't look embarrassed, they looked nervous.

"If you think you may have missed some dirt, I have plenty of time to finish up. There's no sunshine in here at all, so that must mean we have hours until morning. Unless you're blocking the window to keep the sunshine out on purpose. Ha-ha! Why would anyone do that?"

They still didn't smile.

DONG DONG DONG!

"Wait a minute," said Teaflet. "That's the doorbell at the bottom of our tree. No one rings it in the middle of the night. I don't understand."

The clump of creatures began to shuffle away from the window. Shuffle, shuffle, shuffle, they went, every-one together, the bigger ones making sure the littler ones didn't get stepped on.

"What are you doing?" Teaflet had never seen such odd behavior.

Shuffle, shuffle, shuffle. The window was just about to come into view. Shuffle, shuffle, shuffle, shuffle. Then—

DING DING DING!

"And that's the bell at the front door! It must be the

inspector, which means this has to be morning. But why—?"

The shuffling was over, the window was exposed, and Teaflet could now see and understand. There was no sunshine in the room because the window was crammed full of a furry brown nose, one that couldn't come in or pull out. The nose belonged to a baby bear, and he was stuck.

"Uh-oh," said Teaflet.

Like Teaflet, Roog had slept all night on the floor, where he'd fallen in the kitchen. Unlike Teaflet, when the bell went *DONG*, he knew right away that it was

morning and Inspector Maple had arrived. He sprang up in a panic. This was terrible, terrible! He didn't have time to eat breakfast, and no one likes to face a challenge on an empty stomach. Plus, his apron was filthy, splattered with butter, flour, chocolate, and who knew what else.

DING DING DING! Roog had time only to put away the pot holder Teaflet had given him for a pillow before

racing to open the front door.

There she was, the dreaded Inspector Maple, with the even more dreaded neatness list on her clipboard.

"Good morning and welcome, Madam Great and Wise Inspector." Even hungry, Roog had the sense to use flattery.

"You left out Marvelous," she said.

1. BEDS MADE
2. CLOTHES FOLDED
3. TOOTHPASTE ROLLED
4. FLOORS & RUGS.
5. POLISHED POTS.
6. DISHES WASHED.
7. (NO) ANIMALS.
8. (NO) DUST
9. WINDOWS SHINY

He tried again. "Good morning and welcome, Madam Great, Wise, and Marvelous—"

She interrupted. "And Humble."

"Madam Great, Wise, Marvelous, and *Humble* Inspector."

"You are Roog?"

"Yes, I am. Welcome to my spit-spot, fresh-as-a-daisy, scrubbed-to-the-bones home."

"So it's cleaner than you are?"

"Almost anything would be cleaner than I am."

"I agree. According to my records, your sister, Teaflet, lives with you."

"I believe she's taking care of a few last details, Madam Great, Wise, Marvelous, Humble, and All-Knowing Inspector."

"But she's here, in the house?"

"Oh yes," he said. "We'll find her along the way."

He hoped so, anyway. Where *was* Teaflet?

NINE

Teaflet was still in the storage room at the top of the house, trying to free the bear from the window. He hadn't meant to get stuck. He'd been lonely, and had followed the last baby bunny up the stairs. When she fit easily through the window, it didn't occur to him that he might not.

"If we all work together, we can get you out," Teaflet told him. "Now, everybody, line up behind me and, one, two, three, four, FIVE, push!"

Every creature who could push did (the baby bunnies weren't much help), shoving as hard as they could to dislodge the bear. It didn't work.

"Don't lose hope, sweet bear. We'll try again. Everybody, one, two, three, four, five, SIX, push!"

Still nothing.

"This isn't working. I have to think." Teaflet sat down,

then stood right back up before they could knock her over and sit on her. "Let's try this. Everyone who can fit into the wardrobe, hide in there. If the rest of you can be perfectly still when Inspector Maple arrives, maybe she'll think you're statues. And, baby bear, I'll say you're a wall decoration. All right? Go."

While everyone rushed to the wardrobe, Teaflet zipped around the room with her broom, sweeping up whatever the animals had missed. As she worked, she tried to imagine poor Roog handling Inspector Maple on his own. Where in the house were they? Was the in-spection still going on? Or had they already failed?

When she'd gotten every last bit of dirt into the dust-pan, she gave the bear's nose a special kiss.

"Be brave," she whispered. "After the inspection is over, we'll figure out how to get you unstuck. I promise."

She surveyed the room. The wardrobe was full of creatures, with a few paws sticking out. Too many of

them hadn't fit inside, but those left out were practicing standing still. The owl, the toad, and the mouse really did look like statues. The rest were doing the best they could, and it would have to be good enough.

It was the bluebird who pointed out the dustpan problem. The other cleaning supplies were now neatly lined up in a corner, looking as though they belonged there. But that dustpan, and what it contained, was a disaster, and a clue that something was very wrong in the storage room.

"I know what to do." Teaflet sat down on the dustpan, with its dirt, feathers, fur, peach pit, and all. "Now we wait."

TEN

❧*Meanwhile, Roog had* been following Inspector Maple through the house as she peered and pried, stared and stalked, fussed and frowned. It was a terrible experience for him. He was certain that at any minute she'd find a smear on a window or a speck of dust on a table, and put a big *X* on the neatness checklist, and they would have failed the inspection. It wasn't until they reached the third floor without any *X*'s (but where was Teaflet?) and then the fourth (but where was Teaflet?) that he allowed himself to hope. Teaflet had done such a good job of cleaning. They might actually pass.

Now he and Inspector Maple were standing outside the storage room at the top of the house. This was the last part of the house that needed to be inspected. And the last place Teaflet could be. Roog knocked on the door.

"Teaflet, it's me. Are you in there? I'm here with Madam Great, Wise, Marvelous, Humble, All-Knowing, Kind, Splendid . . ." More adjectives had been added during the journey through the house. "I forgot one."

"Brilliant," said Inspector Maple.

"And Brilliant Inspector. Teaflet, she needs to inspect the storage room. If you're in there, may we come in?"

He heard her answer. "Not quite yet, please."

"That's Teaflet," he told Inspector Maple.

"What's she doing?"

"I don't know." Roog wasn't sure he wanted to know. "But we can wait a bit, can't we, Madam Great, Wise, Marvelous, Humble, All-Knowing, Kind, Splendid, Brilliant, and Patient Inspector?"

"I'm not patient. If we're not in that room soon, you'll automatically fail. And you know what that means. You and Teaflet will spend the rest of today cleaning my house."

Roog raised his voice, hoping Teaflet was paying

attention. "Well, I'm sure cleaning your house would be enjoyable."

"No, it wouldn't. I'm giving your sister one minute, beginning"—Inspector Maple set her alarm—"now."

"Did you hear that, Teaflet?" called Roog. "You have just one minute to get ready."

Inside the room, Teaflet was settling herself firmly on the dustpan, and also hoping she wouldn't have to remember all the words in the inspector's extra-long title. Other than that, she wasn't worried. A minute would be plenty of time to turn everyone into statues. But, oh my, the bear did make a peculiar wall decoration.

She whispered, "Everyone, get ready to hold your breath. One, two, three—"

FWOP! The window was suddenly empty! The bear had taken such a big breath, he'd sucked himself free! Teaflet ran over to make sure he was all right. He waved at her, happy to be unstuck, and Teaflet waved back. Now the creatures could leave! Was there still enough time? Yes! In a whirlwind of action, creature after creature flew, leapt, crawled, or bounded through the window. Teaflet threw her cleaning supplies out after them.

She heard Roog call, "Only ten seconds left, Teaflet! TEN!"

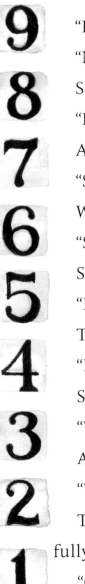

"I'm almost ready!" she called back.

"NINE!" cried Roog.

She tossed the dustpan out the window.

"EIGHT!"

A final look around.

"SEVEN!"

Whoops, there was another baby bunny.

"SIX!"

She helped him out the window.

"FIVE!"

There was *another* one!

"FOUR!"

She put out this baby bunny, too.

"THREE!"

At long last, no more baby bunnies.

"TWO! Teaflet! Please!"

The room was perfectly, absolutely, beautifully clean and tidy.

"ONE!"

"You can come in now!" cried Teaflet.

On the other side of the door, Inspector Maple turned off her alarm and frowned at Roog. "Foiled," she told him. "But maybe not. We have yet to see what your sister has done to the room."

Roog said nothing, as he was wondering that, too. Cautiously, he opened the door and peered inside. Everything looked normal, except for Teaflet, who had confetti stuck to her backside. And except for the raccoon looking in through the window. And the toad?

And a baby *bear*? What had Teaflet been *doing*? Roog made a fearsome face at the raccoon, toad, and bear— and now there was a baby bunny, too—and they ducked out of sight.

He walked into the room, and the inspector stalked in behind him.

"Good morning," said Teaflet brightly. "Welcome to our spit-spot, fresh-as-a-daisy, scrubbed-to-the-bones storage room."

"It had better be all that, young trelf, after you've made me wait."

"Yes, Madam—oh dear, I don't think I can say them all."

"I'll do it," said Roog. "Madam Great, Wise, Marvel-ous, Humble, All-Knowing, Kind, Splendid, Brilliant, and Patient Inspector."

"I've already told you, Roog," said Inspector Maple. "I'm not *patient*."

But she was remarkably patient during her search

through the storage room. Never had Roog or Teaflet endured so thorough an inspection. Not even the hair inspector, who'd gone over every single strand on Roog's head, had taken this much trouble. Inspector Maple looked on top of the wardrobe,

inside the wardrobe, behind the wardrobe, on top of the cupboard, inside the cupboard, behind the cupboard, on top of the boxes, behind the boxes, even inside the boxes, and all over the floor and walls. When she could find nothing wrong, she pulled out a magnifying glass and went over everything again.

By now, Teaflet and Roog were beginning to despair. Anyone who looked that hard and for that long would probably find what she was looking for. Teaflet was about to cry, knowing how sad Roog would be if they failed. Roog was already sad—and crying. Just when the two of them thought they couldn't stand it anymore, Inspector Maple put away her magnifying glass.

"I regret to inform you—"

"I knew it," wept Roog.

"I'm sorry, Roog," wept Teaflet.

"No interruptions, please," said Inspector Maple. "I regret to inform you that my house will not be cleaned today. Despite my long search for a reason to fail you, I've found nothing. Roog and Teaflet, you've passed my inspection."

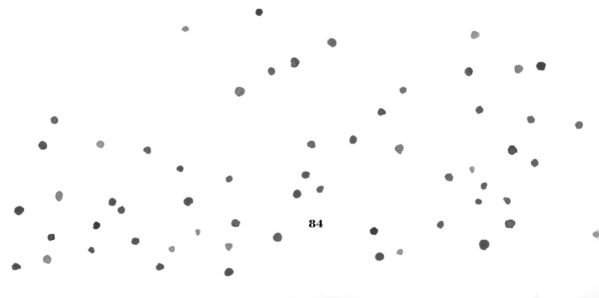

ELEVEN

This morning, I helped Teaflet and Roog get ready for the tenth annual Strawberry Jam Party. Roog didn't let me near the food. (I might have eaten it all.) But I did fold lots of napkins, lots and lots and lots of napkins. While I folded, he told me the whole story of how Teaflet had almost ruined the inspection, and how at first he'd been furious with her. But when she'd told him about the bear stuck in the window, Roog started to laugh, and kept on laughing until he fell on the floor and rolled around for a while. (I laughed, too, though I didn't roll around on the ground. I could have squashed Roog.) By the way, this is a good lesson to learn from Teaflet. If you can make someone laugh, they might forget to be angry with you. Because I'm a grown-up, I *should* tell you it's more important not to make people angry in the first place. Well, none of us is perfect.

TENTH ANNUAL STRAWBERRY JAM PARTY

The party has been going on for hours now. It's a roaring success, the best one ever, even ten times better than the best one ever. Whether it's ten times better than any kind of party, strawberry jam or not, will long be debated throughout Trelfdom.

My folded napkins have gotten several compliments.

The many tables are full of Roog's and Teaflet's friends, plus every creature Teaflet has ever cared for. Inspector Maple is here, too, though neither Teaflet nor Roog remembers inviting her, and I certainly didn't. When she first arrived, she stood off by herself, looking, you know, lonely. I considered saying hello to her to set a good example, but I didn't. The bear is kinder than I am. He lumbered over to introduce himself, and offered to let her scratch his back if she wanted. She didn't, but now I see they are sharing strawberry shortcake and cupcakes. And I think she may have just

smiled at him, but I'm probably wrong about that.

I've been looking for you at the party, but you aren't here. I told Teaflet and Roog you might be along soon. Teaflet was too busy to listen—she was treating the baby hedgehog for sunburn—but I asked Roog to set aside three slices of double-chocolate cake with strawberry jam for you. If you're coming, you should hurry. I'm getting hungry again, and might eat them myself.